Contents

Shivers

BALI RAI

Visit Bali's website
www.balirai.co.uk

First published in 2013 in Great Britain by
Barrington Stoke Ltd
18 Walker Street, Edinburgh, EH3 7LP

www.barringtonstoke.co.uk

ISBN: 978-1-78112-190-0

Printed in China by Leo

Chapter 1

Shivers

The storm came from nowhere.

It was dark and cold, the way Mondays in December should be. The first thing I saw was a single snowflake. A minute later, I couldn't see anything else.

I turned into the estate and saw that the road was deserted. Normally there's at least one crew hanging around. They stand by the big blue bins under the first high rise, and shout at me as I walk home from school. They call me 'geek' and 'gay' and 'little perv' and all kinds of things. My life is like that – no real mates to stand up for me, lots of time on my own. But I'm not bothered, not any more. I'm used to it.

There are normally some adults about on the estate as well. But on that day, there was no one. I was the only loser outside.

My legs started to shake with the cold. The shivers went right up into my chest. I found it hard to breathe. My mum's flat was on the other side of the estate, where it backs onto the rail line. I started to run, in the hope I could get inside before the weather got even worse. It was a stupid thing to do. The soles of my shoes had no grip and I started to slip. The snow was so heavy that it had covered everything in minutes. The parked cars looked like igloos. The little square of grass between the tower blocks was totally white. The sky had this weird orange-red glow, like there was a fire behind the clouds.

I didn't stop running, no matter how much I slid about. The jacket I had on was too thin and it didn't have a hood. My grey school trousers were soaked from the ankle up to my shins. My green bag was heavy with all the books I love to read, and it banged off my back. I was desperate to get inside. I took a left and then a right, into another street. It was also totally deserted. The wind howled and made the snowflakes swirl. The snow had settled in drifts, piled high up every wall and door. I'd never seen anything like it. Crazy.

Home was a hundred metres away still. I started to jog a little faster but I couldn't see a thing. I knew I had to go straight but I couldn't see which way straight was. I wondered why there was so much snow. Where were all the other people? The estate felt creepy and dead. The only noise came from the storm. I couldn't even hear any cars or trains. It was like the world had ended and I was the only one left.

My right knee cracked against a parked car and I felt myself fall, almost in slow-mo. My head smacked against a bin. There was shock and pain, and then I passed out.

I came round to see a girl staring down at me. But she wasn't just any girl. She was the most beautiful girl I'd ever seen. She had bright green eyes and skin so pale that it I could almost see through it. Her hair was the colour of flames.

"Are you hurt?" she asked in a soft, low voice. It was almost a whisper.

"Er ..." I said. I couldn't think straight.

"You've cut your head," she told me.

I rubbed the side of my head as I got to my feet. When I looked at my hand I saw blood. The blood had stained the snow on the ground too. It looked sort of cool, the scarlet on the white. Like the girl's hair against her skin.

"I'm OK," I mumbled. I looked at her. Her eyes seemed to sparkle.

"Do you live near here?" she asked.

"Yeah," I replied. Then I noticed that she wasn't wearing a coat – just dark blue jeans, boots and a grey hooded top. "Aren't you cold?" I asked.

She nodded.

"I'm always cold," she said. "Come on. I'll walk you back to your house."

"Flat," I said.

"I'm sorry?"

"I live in a flat," I told her.

"Right," she said. She held out her hand. My heart jumped. I'd never held a girl's hand before. Never.

"My name's Cassie," she said. "And I don't bite."

I felt myself blush as I took her hand.

"I'm Sam," I said. Her hand was small in mine and felt like a tiny block of ice.

"You need to get some gloves," I said. It was hard not to stare at her. She was gorgeous. Like, if you could have *made* the girl I dreamed of at night, it would have been her.

"I'm used to the cold," she told me. "Come on ..."

Chapter 2

Cassie

The next day I was online when the doorbell rang. When I opened it, Cassie was standing there. Her eyes shone like jewels. My stomach flipped when I saw her and I felt my heart thud.

"No school?" she said, with a smile.

"It's closed because of the snow," I told her.

"Can I come in?"

I nodded and stepped back to let her in. Outside, the estate was deep in snow and deserted.

"Go in there," I told her, and pointed at the living room. The flat I shared with my mum was tiny. There were two bedrooms, a kitchen, a bathroom and the living room. It was painted in a deep maroon colour, which made it feel dark and gloomy. The carpets smelled of dog piss and dirt. I was embarrassed but Cassie didn't seem to notice.

"What are you doing?" she asked, as she sat down on the saggy old sofa.

"Nothing much," I said.

She grinned at me.

"You must be doing *something*," she said. "Even dead people *do* something."

"Like what?" I asked.

"They do being dead." She winked at me.

I saw that she was joking and gave her a half-smile back.

"I was reading a book," I said. "On my computer."

"Was it good?"

I nodded.

"I love books," she told me. She looked away, out the window.

"Me too," I said. I wondered if I should sit down.

"Shall we go for a walk?"

I shrugged and nodded at the grimy window. The sky outside was iron-grey.

"It's freezing out there," I pointed out.

"So?" she replied. "YOLO."

"Huh?"

She grinned at me and her whole face seemed to light up.

"You only live once?"

I cussed myself for being so stupid – of course I knew what YOLO meant. Cassie had on the same jeans, boots and top as the previous day.

"Haven't you got a jacket or something?" I asked her.

"No," she said, and looked away. "I haven't got much."

I decided not to push it any further. It was clear she didn't mind the cold, or she wouldn't want to go out in the snow.

"OK then," I told her. "But I'm gonna get a hat. Do you want my scarf?"

Cassie nodded.

"If you insist," she said. "Don't want you to worry that I'll die of frostbite or anything."

The estate was deserted again and we made for a small park, close to the main road. I planned to take her the long way round because I wanted to avoid the bullies who hung around the bins. Cassie stopped.

"Why don't we go that way?" she asked, and pointed down past the first high rise on the estate.

I thought fast about how to reply.

"Er … why hurry?" I said. "We've got all day."

Cassie seemed happy with that. As we walked she told me about one of her favourite books. I couldn't take my eyes from her face as I listened. A couple of times I almost bumped into things, but I didn't care. She was amazing.

"Tell me about one of your favourites now," she said.

"Huh?"

"Your favourite books," she said. "Tell me about one of them."

"Er ..."

Cassie giggled and pinched my arm. It was so light that I hardly felt it. It was like being touched by a butterfly or something. I wondered what it would be like to kiss her.

"I hope you weren't lying to me," she joked. "You told me that you love books."

"I do," I protested. "I just can't think of one right now."

"Is that cos you're too busy looking at me?" she asked, with a sly smile.

I felt myself turn red as I tried to grin back. Cassie's face changed. She looked worried.

"I didn't mean to make fun of you," she told me. "I like it."

"Like what?" I asked.

"I like that you like looking at me," she said.

10

The sky was heavy and grey above us, and the ice-cold wind cut into the skin on my face. But even though I was freezing, being with Cassie made me happier than I'd been in years.

"Come on, weirdo," she said, "let's get to the park before we turn into ice cubes."

Chapter 3
The Park

A little brook runs through the middle of the park and under the main road. There's a path beside the brook that goes into a narrow tunnel under the road and then comes out between rows of houses on the other side. The tunnel is closed off, with danger signs everywhere, but Cassie ignored them and headed that way.

I knew why the tunnel was closed. It was a place I wanted to avoid.

"Stop, Cassie," I said. "They wouldn't close the tunnel if there wasn't something wrong with it."

"It's fine," she told me. "I used to walk under there all the time."

I looked down the small bank to the snowy path, and shook my head.

"I don't want to go down there," I said.

"Why not?"

I thought back to what had happened when I was younger and shook my head. "Don't want to say."

Cassie seemed irritated and I started to worry that she'd leave me there and go away. But in the end she just smiled and took my hand.

"OK," she said. "Shall we go on the swings?"

I nodded and we walked on. I wondered whether I should explain more about the tunnel.

"Er ... it's not that I'm scared," I told her, "to go down to the tunnel, I mean."

Cassie shook her head.

"You don't have to tell me," she said. She looked right into my eyes. I turned away and shook my head.

"I *do* have to tell you," I said. "Everyone else thinks I'm a freak and I don't want you to think that too."

We had reached the swings and I brushed the snow from the seats. I took a yellow swing and Cassie sat on a red one.

"I don't think you're a freak," she told me. "I don't know you very well, but I like what I've seen so far."

"You do?"

Cassie nodded.

"Something horrible happened down there," I said. "In the tunnel under the road."

"What happened?" she asked.

"Someone died and there was lots of fuss and it was ..."

I stopped myself and gulped down air. I was being stupid. Why was I telling her anything at all? I knew that Cassie was beautiful and the only friend I'd had in years, but I didn't really know her at all.

"It's OK," she said, like she had read my mind. "You can trust me, Sam."

"But I don't even know who you are," I said. "You say you used to go into the tunnel all the time, but I've never seen you around here before."

"I used to live over the road," she told me. "But then I ... I moved on."

"Oh."

"And sometimes I come back – that's all. I miss it. I miss my old friends too, but they've forgotten about me."

I looked at her bright green eyes and fiery hair and wondered how anyone could ever forget her.

"I bet they haven't forgotten," I said.

Cassie shook her head sadly.

"Trust me," she said. "They've moved on too."

We sat in silence for a while and then I got up and pushed Cassie's swing for her.

"Fantasy or reality?" she asked me.

"I don't understa – "

"Books," she cut in. "Which do you prefer? Fantasy or reality?"

I thought about it and shook my head.

"I like both," I said. "Like, there's times when I like fantasy. When I want to escape and that. Then there's times when I want to read about people like me, doing real stuff."

Cassie giggled again.

"But you have to pick one," she said. "Or else the game doesn't work."

"OK," I said. "Fantasy."

"Why?"

I thought a bit more before I replied.

"Because you can go anywhere in a fantasy," I told her.

"Unless your real life became a fantasy," she pointed out.

I shook my head.

"But it can't, can it?" I asked. "I mean real life is just ... *real*."

"Not all the time," Cassie said. "Did you know that there's ships that have been found in the sea with all of their crew missing? No one knows where the people went."

16

I nodded.

"Ships like the Mary Celeste," I said.

Cassie shook her head.

"That's an old story," she said. "I mean things that have happened in the last few years. Things no one can explain. That's real life and fantasy in one ..."

"I haven't heard any stories like that."

"We'll look them up," she told me. "On your computer."

I felt my insides grow warmer.

"You're coming round again?" I asked.

Cassie stopped the swing and turned to look at me.

"Try and stop me, Sam. I like you."

That night I couldn't sleep. Cassie's voice, her eyes, her lips swam around inside my head. Everything. I imagined kissing her and touching her and my brain almost went into overload. I turned on my laptop and googled pictures of red-haired girls and every one I saw reminded me of Cassie in some way.

But Cassie reminded me of herself too – does that makes sense? It was like I knew her before I met her. Like she'd been around for years. I felt so easy around her, and I didn't get that with anyone else except my mum.

By the time I stopped looking at my laptop, it was after five in the morning. My eyes felt like they had been rubbed with sandpaper. But even then I couldn't get her out of my mind ...

Chapter 4

Problems

I spent the next few days at home as school was still closed. The cold weather just got worse and my mum moaned about having to walk to work because the buses weren't running.

"It's mad," she said. "You'd think they could clear the roads."

I was eating toast and peanut butter and wondering when Cassie would come round.

"What have you been doing with your time off?" Mum asked me.

"Nothing much," I said. "I've not got any homework and there's nothing much going on."

She looked at me and smiled.

"Try and go out," she said. "You can't stay cooped up in here all day."

"I have been out," I told her.

"Good. At the weekend we'll do something, OK?"

I shrugged. "I'm not ten years old any more, Mum. You don't have to do stuff with me just cos you think I might get bored."

She shook her head and set down her coffee mug.

"That's not why I do it," she said. "We should spend time together – that's what parents and kids do. I know things haven't been easy since ..."

I watched her face turn red and then she swallowed like there was a lump in her throat. I knew that she was going to cry. I didn't say anything.

"See you later," she said at last. Then she rushed out to work.

I sat and thought about what had happened to our family. How we'd supported my dad through a big mess he'd been in, only for him to leave us as soon as he was sorted. And he left us in a total mess, with no money and stuck on this grotty estate. I was only in Year 5 when it all happened but I wasn't stupid. I knew that my dad was a waste of space.

I was still thinking about my dad when Cassie turned up.

"You OK?" she asked, as soon as I let her in.

"Yeah," I said. I didn't mean it.

Cassie could see I was in a state. She asked if I wanted to talk.

"It's ..." I began to try to tell her about it, but then I started to cry. I got angry with myself for being such a baby and that made me cry even more. I only stopped when Cassie kissed me.

"Sssh ..." she whispered.

The touch of her lips lingered on mine. The kiss was ice cold and sweet, but it was so light that it felt like it wasn't real. I stopped crying and wiped my eyes on the sleeve of my top.

"Tell me," she said. "That's what friends are for."

"Is it?" I asked. "I don't have any friends."

"Apart from me," she said.

I nodded, and felt myself break into a little smile.

"Apart from you," I repeated.

When I was a kid my dad had been a science teacher. We'd lived in a different part of the city, in a nice house with a garden and lovely neighbours. I grew up around books and music and that's why I love them both now. My parents seemed to get on fine but then one day everything changed. I was about eight. I heard them arguing in the kitchen. I walked in and my mum was crying. She took me by the hand and said I had to go to my room. When I asked what was wrong, she just shook her head and told me not to worry.

That night the police came to our house and took my dad away. He looked angry and upset and kept on telling them they had made a mistake. But the police took him anyway and my mum just sat and cried. My dad was away for a long time. Any time mum and me went to the shops or the cinema, people would shout at us and swear. I didn't know why they were doing it but it really got to my mum and she got really depressed. Then, about a year after my dad was taken away, we had to leave our house. My mum promised me it would be like an adventure, and we packed some of our stuff into boxes. That's how we ended up on the estate, stuck in our crappy flat.

At first it wasn't too bad because no one knew us, so people didn't shout at us in the street. But soon that changed and my mum started to get sad again. Some of the older lads started to call me names and no one would be my friend. I got bullied and beaten up and had things thrown at me – and all because of my dad.

I mean, I don't think my dad *did* anything. The police didn't charge him and he didn't go to jail. It was all a big mistake. But even after he was released, people were still mean to Mum and me. I still got loads of grief – like the lads who called me names and bullied me. That's how it's been ever since. Only now we can't move again because we've got no money. So we're stuck and my dad has just abandoned us, even though he's not in trouble any more and everything is OK. I don't even know what he does any more. See, it might be fine for him but it's not fine for us. I hate him.

When I finished telling Cassie all this, she held my hand.

"Do you still see your dad?" she asked.

I shook my head.

"I don't even want to see him," I told her. "He's a bastard."

"Don't you miss him?"

I shook my head.

"I was only little when he went," I said. "And he's never even sent me a birthday card since."

"Are you like him – like, do you *look* like him?"

I shrugged. "Dunno," I said. "And I don't care either. Why do you want to know?"

Cassie shrugged back at me.

"No reason," she told me. "What about the bullies – do they hang around on the estate?"

I nodded. "You know how we took the long way round, to get to the park?" I said.

Cassie nodded.

"That's why," I told her. "The worst one is called Danny Simms." I rolled up the left leg of my jeans.

Cassie gasped when she saw the scar on my shin. It was about two inches long and thick.

"What the ...?"

"It was a broken bottle," I told her. "Simms told me that if I told anyone he'd kill my mum. I pretended that I'd scraped my leg falling off a wall."

"Oh my God!" Cassie said.

"He takes my money too," I told her.

Her face changed and I could see that she was angry. "How old is he?" she asked.

"Dunno – he's not at school any more, so he's maybe about seventeen?"

"He's two years older than you!" Cassie sounded really angry now.

I shrugged and rolled my jeans down again.

"We're gonna get him." Cassie said.

I felt my stomach sink and I shook my head. "How can we *get* him?" I asked. "He'll just beat us up."

Cassie looked into my eyes.

"Do you trust me?" she asked.

I nodded.

"So if I tell you we can get Danny Simms, you believe me, OK?"

"But ..."

Cassie told me she had to go.

"But I thought we were going to ..." I began. She cut me off.

"I'll be back tomorrow – promise," she said, in a stern voice that made me nervous.

"OK," I mumbled. I wished that I hadn't told her about the bully. He would kill me for sure.

"But there's one thing, Sam," Cassie added. "If I help you, then you have to promise to help me."

"Help you do what?"

Cassie shook her head.

"You have to promise, and not ask any questions."

"But ..."

"Just listen, Sam!" she shouted. Her face was even paler and her eyes blazed with anger.

She startled me. I shrugged and moved away from her.

"Sorry, Sam," said Cassie. "I didn't mean to shout. But if I get rid of your problem with Danny Simms, for good, will you help me?"

I thought about my life without the bullies in it and how much easier it would be.

"OK," I said.

"No questions asked?"

"Agreed."

Cassie leant over and placed another kiss on my lips. It felt as strange as the first one – almost as light as air.

"I'll be back tomorrow," she said.

Now I look back, I should have seen what was happening. Cassie had me in a spell and I was blind. Maybe if I hadn't been so into her, things would have been different. I didn't know it at the time, but being with Cassie was going to turn my whole world to crap ...

Chapter 5
The Attack

Cassie turned up at lunchtime.

"Get your coat," she said.

I looked at the thick snowflakes falling from the white sky. "Where are we going?"

"To see Danny Simms," she replied.

I wanted to turn around, shut the door and go back to bed but I didn't. I was scared, but I wanted to see what Cassie would do. I wanted to see how she would stop Danny from bullying me. So I got my coat and put it on. When I asked her what she had planned, Cassie just shook her head.

"Just wait until we get there."

"Where?"

Cassie told me to hurry up. "Simms is by the bins," she told me. "Him and his mates are throwing snowballs at anyone they see."

"But what if he gets angry?" I asked, as I closed the front door behind me.

"Let him," she said. "I want him to get angry."

We took the stairs down to the ground floor because the lift was broken. Outside the snow was even thicker but this time there were a few people around. I guessed that they had got tired of waiting for the snow to stop. They were trying to get on with things, like my mum.

"Bloody weather," I mumbled.

Cassie smiled at me. "I like it," she said.

We walked across the estate until we were round the corner from Danny and his mates. I could hear them shouting and swearing, and my heart began to beat faster. I felt sick.

"Whatever happens," Cassie told me, "you just do what I say. OK?"

"But ..."

"Sam – just listen to me and everything will be fine."

"He's gonna batter me," I mumbled.

Cassie shook her head. "No he won't," she said. "I won't let him."

She told me to walk round the corner and call Danny names.

"No matter *what* he says or does, you don't listen," she said. "Understood?"

"Understood."

I took a deep breath and walked over to the bins. Danny was sitting on one, and he grinned when he saw me.

"Hello gay boy!" he shouted. He turned to his mates. "Look who's come out to play!"

I turned round to see what Cassie was doing but she'd gone. My stomach sank and I felt my legs start to shake. Where was she? I heard Danny jump down from the blue bin behind me.

"Who you looking for?" he asked me. "Your mum?"

I faced him again and fought to find my breath.

"No," I said, in the loudest voice I could manage. "I'm looking for your mum. I've got a fiver and I'm after a good time."

Both Danny's mates began to snigger under the scarves they'd tied round the bottom part of their faces. All three of them were wearing hooded tops, with caps over the top.

"Nah!" one of them said. "The man's cussing you, Danny!"

"Bust him in the mouth!" said the other one.

I looked past them, to where I hoped to see Cassie. Not that she could help when Danny was this angry. He balled his hands into fists and began to walk towards me.

"You what?" he asked. "You talking about my mum?"

I shrugged and went for it.

"Yeah," I said, even though my voice was shaky and I felt sweat on my forehead.

"You're dead!" he yelled.

I wanted to run away back to my bedroom, but I was frozen. He was less than five feet away from me and I couldn't move. I saw him pull back his right arm and make a fist inside his leather glove. I closed my eyes, ready for the pain. But nothing happened – at least, not to *me*.

"*ARRGH!*" I heard Danny yelp.

I opened my eyes and saw him standing on the spot, rubbing his head. Cassie stood behind him, holding a piece of metal pipe. Danny span round to see who had hit him and I shut my eyes. I was waiting for Cassie to get punched too but then things went crazy ...

Danny lashed out, but it was like he couldn't even see Cassie. She stepped to one side and hit him again. He screamed in agony and fell to his knees. The pipe had cut his left cheek and blood dripped from the wound. I looked at his mates and they had stopped grinning and joking. Now they both stood in shock, like they couldn't believe what they were seeing.

Danny got up and lashed out again, and again he missed Cassie.

"What's goin' on!" he shouted. "What the ...?"

Cassie smacked him on his nose and I heard it break. Her eyes were wide with rage. She hit him on the left temple and then in the stomach. Danny fell back and landed in the snow. His hands were at his face and he was in tears.

"What the ...?"

"RUN!" I heard his mates cry out.

I watched Danny's mates disappear into the tower block, leaving him behind. I couldn't work out what was happening. My head was spinning. Why had Danny just let Cassie hit him with the pipe? And why were his mates running away like they'd seen a ghost?

"Take it!" I heard Cassie order. She held out the pipe to me.

"But ..."

"*Sam!*" She almost growled my name.

I walked over to her and took the pipe, and then I turned to face Danny. His eyes grew wide and he started to sob.

"D ... don't," he begged.

"Hit him," said Cassie.

"But I can't ..." I told her. "I can't just hit him when he's lying there and bleeding ..."

Danny's eyes grew even wider still and he looked like he was in shock.

"Who ...?" he began to mumble. "What ... are you *crazy*, bruv?"

Cassie took hold of my arm.

"*HIT HIM!!!!*" she hissed. "Go on!"

I lifted the pipe into the air, closed my eyes and did as she said.

"*Again! Again! Again!*" she screamed.

When I was finished, Danny was out cold on the ground. The snow had turned scarlet and his face was a bloody mess. The pipe was on the ground. And Cassie ...

Cassie had vanished ...

Chapter 6
Results

The police turned up some time the following afternoon. I was in my bedroom, trying to work out what had happened. I'd been up all night wondering where Cassie had gone. I was worried sick that Danny might be dead. Danny was a bully but that didn't mean I wanted to kill him. I just wanted him to stop hurting me all the time.

When I opened the door and saw the police, I thought I would have a heart attack.

"Hello, son, are your mum or dad at home?" the male copper asked.

"At work," I heard myself reply, my mind racing.

The other copper was female and she smiled at me, but not in a kind way.

"When will they be back?" she asked.

I shrugged and looked down at my feet. "Dunno. Mum's at work."

"You've already told us that," she said. "What time does she get home?"

"About s-six," I stammered.

"OK. We'll be back later, then," she replied. "There's been an attack on the estate and we're looking for witnesses."

I felt my mouth go dry but I knew that I had to look at the policewoman. If I didn't she'd think I was guilty – that's what happened in all the crime novels I read. I lifted my head and tried to stay calm.

"I've been in all day," I said.

"We can't ask you anything without your mum here," the male copper told me.

"Who got attacked?" I asked.

"We can't say, son – but it's bad," he replied. "We'll come back this evening. Let your mum know we've been, OK?"

"Yeah ..." I said. I closed the door on them and ran back to my bedroom.

I paced around for a while, wishing that Cassie was with me. Then I started to feel sick again and I got into bed. The policeman had said it was bad – that had to mean that Danny was dead or something. What if someone had seen me?

Would I have to go to jail?

And *where* was Cassie?

My mum came home just after six and I told her that the police had come round. I wanted to tell her everything else too but I couldn't. In the end I didn't have time anyway. The police knocked on the door about fifteen minutes after Mum got back.

"Is your mum in?" the female copper asked as soon as I opened the door. Her face was stern and she was glaring into my eyes. I felt sick and looked down at my feet. I realised that I was in real trouble. They must have been waiting, watching the flat – ready for when my mum came home.

I nodded.

"Who's that?" my mum called from the kitchen.

The female copper didn't wait for me to reply.

"Detective Sergeant Mirza," she said. "Could my partner and I come in?"

She walked in without waiting for answer and her partner followed her. Both were wearing normal clothes and the man looked even more stern than the woman. My mum came into the tiny hall, looking worried.

"Is something wrong?" she asked.

DS Mirza looked at her partner.

"DS Webb," the man said, getting his ID card out. "We should sit down."

Mum showed them into the living room and began to tidy things away. I could tell that she was embarrassed by the state of our flat. The coppers sat down next to each other on the sofa. I stood at the window with my head down.

"No need to do that, Mrs Taylor," said DS Mirza. "Please sit down."

My mum shot her a dirty look.

"It's not *Taylor!*" she snapped, her face going red. "I'm using my own surname now – Bains."

"I'm sorry if I caused any offence," said DS Mirza.

"What's this about?" my mum asked.

DS Webb cleared his throat.

"A teenager was attacked on the estate yesterday," he said. "We think Sam was involved."

I felt my stomach flip and I wanted to run out of the room. But I froze and stayed where I was, not looking at anyone.

"*My* Sam?" said Mum. "Are you having a laugh?"

"No," said DS Webb. "I'm very serious. We have witnesses who place Sam at the scene. We may also have CCTV footage of the attack."

"You may?"

DS Webb nodded.

"We've had to get a court order to view it," DS Mirza said. "Should be with us tonight."

I looked up and saw my mum's caramel skin grow paler. She turned to me.

"Sam?" she asked.

I kept my eyes on hers and said nothing.

"Sam!" she repeated.

"I didn't touch anyone," I mumbled.

"We need you to come with us," said DS Mirza. "We have to ask Sam some questions."

"Ask them here, then," my mum said.

"I'm not sure you understand," said DS Webb. "We're arresting Sam for attempted murder, Ms Bains."

"But ..." she began.

"I didn't touch him!" I shouted. I wished I'd never listened to Cassie. I wished that she was in the room with us. Not that it mattered. If they *did* have CCTV or witnesses, they'd know about Cassie too.

"*Him?*" replied DS Mirza. "How did you know it was a male?"

"Mum ...?" I pleaded.

"Is there anyone you need to call? A lawyer, perhaps?" DS Mirza asked.

"My brother," said Mum. "I need to call my brother."

"OK," DS Mirza said. "Please do that now and then we'll take you both to the station."

"If you don't have a lawyer," DS Webb added, "we can get you the phone number for one when we get to the station."

"My brother *is* a lawyer," my mum told them.

DS Webb turned to me.

"Sam Taylor, I'm arresting you on suspicion of attempted murder ..."

I didn't hear the rest because I puked my guts up.

Chapter 7
Cassie's Return

We got back from the police station just after midnight. My mum asked me if I was hungry and I told her no.

"I just want to go to sleep," I said.

"Did you do what they said?" she asked.

"No, Mum," I lied, just as I'd done with the police.

"Well, in that case we'll be OK," she said.

"You should go to bed," I told her. "You'll be tired for work."

She yawned and nodded. "I'll speak to you tomorrow, OK?" she said.

"Yeah," I said, and went into my bedroom.

The police had waited for my uncle to arrive before they asked me anything. My uncle sat with me through all of the questions. Before they started he got to talk to me in private for five minutes. He asked if I was guilty and I lied to him. I told him that I had no idea why they'd arrested me. In the interview room, the police kept on talking about witnesses and video evidence but I kept my mouth shut. It was something I'd read about in all the detective stories I'd read. If I kept my mouth shut, they couldn't do anything. If they really did have all that evidence, I would get done anyway. Why make things easy for them?

But the thing is, I felt really guilty. I wanted to know what had happened to Danny but they wouldn't say. They asked over and over again how I'd known the victim was male before they told me. I told them that some lads had been talking about the attack, but I couldn't remember who they were. I didn't mention Cassie once. I was angry with her for leaving me to deal with everything but I didn't want her to get into trouble. I just wanted to know where she was.

In the end DS Webb turned up and told DS Mirza something in private. Her face fell as she listened and they left the room. When they came back in, my uncle asked if they were charging me with anything. DS Mirza said that they weren't. She told me that I was still under suspicion but that they needed to make further enquiries.

"No evidence," my uncle had said afterwards. "So much for their witnesses then."

I woke up just as my mum walked into my room the following morning.

"I haven't checked if school is open," she said, with a yawn.

"It's Saturday, mum," I reminded her.

"Already?" she said. "Are you doing anything today?"

I shook my head.

"I don't want to go out," I told her. "Not after what happened."

"Are you sure you don't know anything?" she asked.

"MUM!" I shouted.

"I'll be back around six, then," she said. "Call me if you need anything."

"OK."

As soon as she left, I went back to sleep, and I only woke up again when I heard someone banging on the front door. I thought it would be the police again, and so I put on my jeans and a hooded top before I answered it.

It was Cassie. "Hey!" she said, with a huge smile.

She looked even more pale and fragile than before and she had on the same clothes.

"Hey," I said, my voice flat.

"You going to ask me in then?"

I shrugged. "I got arrested," I told her. "Because of what happened."

Cassie nodded. "I know," she said. "I was watching you."

I screwed up my face as a blast of icy wind made me shiver. "You were *watching*?"

"Let me in and I'll explain," she said, smiling again.

I told her to come in but didn't smile back. I went into the bathroom to clean my teeth and Cassie followed me in. It was tight enough in there with one person. With her squeezed in too, there was no room to move. Cassie smelled of cut grass and something else – earth, maybe. It sounds like a nasty smell but it wasn't. It was sort of fresh, if that makes sense.

"Can't clean my teeth with you watching," I told her.

She grinned at me in the mirror, but her reflection seemed to wobble in the steam coming from the hot tap. I wiped the mirror as she left.

"They can't get you," she told me through the open door.

I had already put the toothbrush in my mouth so I didn't reply.

"Charming," she said, in a sulky voice. "I'll be in your bedroom."

I finished my teeth and shut the door to go to the toilet. When I came out, Cassie was waiting for me.

"It's your turn now," she told me.

"My turn for what?" I asked. "I'm about to eat my breakfast."

"To help me," she said. "It's your turn to help me."

I shook my head.

"I have to eat first," I said. "Are you hungry?"

"I don't really eat," she told me. "Never did."

I shook some cereal into a bowl, added some milk and grabbed a spoon.

"In the living room," I said, wondering if she'd realise that I was unhappy with her.

"I'm sorry," she said, almost as soon as I'd had the thought.

"No, you're not," I shot back. "You don't even look bothered."

Cassie went to the window and looked out at the grey skies.

"I am," she insisted. "Please believe me."

I ate some cereal and so I didn't have to reply for a bit. Cassie kept her back to me, humming some tune I didn't recognise.

When I'd eaten a bit more I asked her where she'd disappeared to after we'd attacked Danny.

"I couldn't stay," she told me. "It's complicated."

"But you left me there," I reminded her. "Was it OK for *me* to stay?"

She shook her head. "You don't understand," she said. "But you will, I promise. Once you've helped me."

She wasn't making any sense. "Helped you with what?" I asked, raising my voice.

Cassie turned to face me and I could see that she'd been crying.

"I didn't want to leave you, Sam," she insisted. "I *had* to."

"I'm sorry," I said, feeling bad about making her cry. "I didn't mean to ..."

"I'm the reason you didn't get charged," she stated.

"Huh?"

"By the police," she said. "I got rid of the CCTV evidence ..."

I put my bowl on the small table in front of me. My mum's coffee mug was still sitting there, half-full.

"How could you do that?" I asked. "How did you ...?"

"There's a security office on the estate," she explained. "I broke in and turned off the cameras."

Something didn't make sense and it was doing my head in.

"But what about Danny's mates?" I asked her. "They saw us ..."

Cassie shook her head.

"They won't say anything," she told me. Her face was serious and her green eyes burned into mine.

"But ..."

"Sam," she said sternly. "Trust me – they won't say anything. If they were going to, you would have been charged by now."

I shook my head.

"I didn't want to hurt him," I told her. "I didn't want that."

"I know," she said. She came over and joined me on the sofa. She placed a hand on my arm. It felt lighter than air.

"He would have come after you," she said. "I had to stop him. *We* had to stop him. Don't you see?"

"But we nearly killed him," I said. "The police said that it was attempted murder."

"And what about your leg?" she reminded me. "What was that – a *game*?"

"But ..."

"*NO!*" she shouted, making me flinch. "People who hurt other people can't be allowed to get away with it. Not ever!"

"But we hurt him back," I said. "That makes us as bad as him, doesn't it?"

"No, it doesn't," she said, more calmly. "We were defending you, Sam. *From* him. It's not the same thing."

"But when he wakes up, he'll say it was us," I pointed out. "And we'll still get into trouble."

"No." She didn't blink. "He *won't* wake up."

I gulped down air and felt my head start to spin.

"But if he dies ..."

"People who hurt other people *deserve* to die," she said.

I didn't agree with her but I didn't know how to say it. She was so sure about it all. And I didn't want her to hate me, even though she'd upset me. She was the only friend I'd ever really had.

"Someone like Danny hurt me," she whispered. "Somebody cruel and evil and full of hate."

"Who?" I whispered back. Now I was beginning to understand why she was so angry.

"Someone," she replied. "He got away with it, too."

I looked into her face and saw that she had dirt streaked across the back of her neck and her clothes were stained. I wondered where she went when she wasn't with me. Was she homeless or something?

"Are you sure you're OK?" I asked her. "Do you want, like, a bath or something?"

Cassie looked at her grubby hands and then at me.

"I suppose I am a bit dirty," she said. "But I don't care. I don't care about anything except getting *him*."

"Who?" I asked.

"The man," she whispered again. "The one who ..."

I felt something inside me begin to tear open. It was like there was this box that held my anger inside it. I thought about someone touching Cassie, hurting her, and I started to get really mad.

"Is that what you need my help with?" I asked her.

"Yes," she said. "And I haven't got much time left. We have to get him soon."

"Why?"

She shook her head sadly.

"You'll understand," she explained. "I promise, Sam. Soon ..."

I started to say something but then she kissed me. Her lips were cold and tasted of something I couldn't place. I put my hands around her shoulders. They were just skin and bone and they felt like they might break in my grip. The cut-grass smell of her hair got stronger.

"Close your eyes," she whispered.

"Huh?"

"Close your eyes," she repeated. "Don't open them for anything. Promise?"

"Why not?"

Cassie touched my face.

"Please, Sam. Trust me ..."

I was about to shrug but I held off. I was sick of never knowing. The most beautiful girl I had

ever seen was kissing me. She was telling me
to close my eyes and I was asking questions. I
cussed myself and did as she asked.

"Lie back," she told me. "And keep your eyes
closed ..."

This time I didn't reply. I just did as she
asked. She ran her hands down my chest,
towards the belt of my jeans. My belly started
to churn and I felt hot all over. As she undid my
jeans, I thought my heart was going to burst out
of my chest. I froze, unsure of what to do next.

"Cassie ... I ..."

"Sssshhh!!!!" I heard her whisper, over and
over again.

Chapter 8
The Plan

Cassie told me her plan afterwards.

"He lives on another estate," she said. "The one opposite the football ground?"

"I know it," I told her, only I couldn't look her in the eye. Not after what we'd just done. What she'd just done. I was embarrassed. I'd never felt anything like it. It was like I'd had the maddest dream and then woken up. Only it hadn't been a dream because Cassie was right there, and I could still feel her touching me.

"He goes to work – driving a taxi," she said. "He'll be out."

"What – we need to go now?"

Cassie nodded.

"Why aren't you looking at me?" she asked.

I was going to lie to her but something stopped me. I decided to be honest instead.

Cassie listened to me and then sort of smiled. "I like you, Sam," she said. "You're not like him."

"Like who?" I asked, confused again.

"The one who hurt me," she said.

"But why would I be like him?"

Cassie went back over to the window.

"No reason," she mumbled. "I'm just ... I need to rest, Sam. And I can't do that if he's out there, getting away with it. He might hurt someone else too."

"What do you want me to do?" I asked, deciding that I would help after all.

Cassie turned to me and smiled. "Thank you," she said. But her eyes didn't smile along with her mouth. They just looked sad.

"I'm not hitting him or anything," I told her. "Not like Danny. I won't do that again."

Cassie nodded. "I promise you won't have to hit him," she told me. "We just need to get something from his flat."

"His flat?"

She nodded again.

"Don't worry," she said. "He won't be there. You just have to break in and take what I want and that's it."

I started to feel uneasy. What did I know about breaking in to flats? I wasn't a thief.

"But how do I get in?" I asked her.

Cassie came and sat down and explained everything to me. When she was done, she took my hand.

"Do you promise?" she asked, looking into my eyes. "Please, Sam."

"I really, really like you," I said. "You know I do."

"So promise," she repeated.

"Are we, like, together, then?" I asked. "Like you're my girlfriend?"

Cassie half-smiled. "If you want me to be," she replied.

"And if I do this – is that it? No more dodgy stuff?"

She nodded. "Promise," she said. "After this, I won't ask you for anything else, ever."

"OK then," I told her. "I'll do it."

The flat Cassie wanted me to break into had a grubby, stained door with peeling blue paint, and a panel of glass in the middle. I stood on the landing and tried not to panic. I was alone. Cassie had gone off again, telling me that she had something else to do and would see me back at my mum's. I wasn't happy, but I'd agreed to break in on my own. I waited a few moments, just to be sure that no one would appear. There were ten doors on the landing, five on each side. That was nine other residents who might catch me at any time. As fast as I could, I took the small hammer I'd borrowed from my mum's toolkit, wrapped the head of it in my scarf and broke the glass. I held my breath.

The scarf muffled the sound of the glass but my heart still beat faster and I still expected someone to catch me at any moment. But when no doors opened, I calmed down a bit. I reached through the hole and tried to find the handle. I was wearing my gloves and had my hood pulled up over a beanie hat. If anyone did see me, they'd call the police for sure.

At last I found the handle and the skanky door fell open. I darted inside and shut the door behind me. The flat was even smaller than ours, with one small hallway, and three doors leading from it. I opened the first one and saw a tiny bathroom, which stank. On the other side there was a kitchen, with just enough space for a cooker, a small fridge, and a worktop. The sink was coated in grime and there were empty fast-food cartons piled up on the floor. It smelled worse than the bathroom. The last door was a combined bed and living room, with two big windows that looked out over the city. The floor was covered in a nasty brown carpet, and the bed was unmade. Three ashtrays sat on a small wooden table, each of them overflowing with butts. There was an old telly, a mini stereo and a pile of clothes as well. It was nasty. Whoever lived in the flat was a lazy, dirty slob.

Cassie had told me that the thing I was to get was taped to the back of the cooker. I went into the kitchen, kicked the empty food cartons away, and looked at it. It was covered in a layer of grease and something furry and mouldy sat in one corner. I began to pull it away from the wall, glad that I had gloves on.

It took a few goes but at last the cooker came forwards. A load of cockroaches scuttled out from their hiding place under the bottom. I ignored them and leant over it, but I couldn't see anything. There was a pipe and a wire, but nothing else.

I leaned further across to look again, and the grease got onto my jeans. And that's when I saw it, right down at the base of the cooker. A plastic bag like you get at the supermarket. I reached down and pulled it away, standing right on my toes. It came free after a couple of tugs and I stood up. I wanted to see what was in it but I decided to wait until I got back. I shoved the package under my top, pushed the cooker back and left the flat. My heart was racing now and I could hear the blood pumping around my head. I had to hurry.

Back on the landing, I shut the door as quietly as I could. Suddenly I heard a voice – a man. Then one of the other doors began to open. Panicked, I sprinted towards the stairs and only just made it. The man's voice was followed by a woman's – both of them speaking in loud African accents. I ran down all ten flights of stairs, until I was outside in the snow again. There were very few people around and I set off for the bus stop, praying that I wouldn't get caught. The bus turned up soon and before I knew it, I was back on my own estate.

But when I got home, Cassie hadn't come back. I waited for her to show up, but she didn't. By the time my mum got back from work, I had realised that she wasn't coming.

Chapter 9
Nightmares

All day Sunday and into the week, I heard nothing from Cassie. I started to get worried that she had been hurt. Maybe the man whose flat I'd broken into had got her. Maybe a car had hit her or one of Danny Simms' crew had beaten her up. All sorts of things went through my head and I felt like I was going mad. School opened again, so I was out of the flat all day. Even if Cassie had come to see me, I wouldn't have been in. It was Wednesday evening before I decided that I had to go and look for her.

I went down to the park first, but it was deserted apart from some lads chucking ice at each other. The fence by the path to the brook had fallen down. I walked over, hoping that Cassie might be there. There was no sign of her. I thought about following the path under the road but decided not to. It was freezing and to be honest, I was still a bit scared of going down there.

I turned back, and walked the streets around the estate for an hour. Then I went up to the High Street. It was packed with people and traffic and the noise made me nervous. I didn't find her.

Back at the flat, my mum had made sausage and mash. I wasn't hungry and it felt like I was swallowing bricks. Luckily my mum didn't notice. Then her sister rang and she had to go out.

"I'll be about an hour," she told me. "Finish up and wash the dishes for me, OK?"

"Sure, Mum," I said.

After I'd dumped my dinner and cleaned up, I went into my bedroom and turned on my laptop. I sat and surfed the Net, not looking at anything in particular. A couple of people had put messages on Facebook about Danny Simms but there was nothing about me. On YouTube, I watched a girl with weird bendy legs on one of those talent shows. Then I watched a couple of music videos. But all the time, the only thing I could think about was Cassie. I couldn't believe she'd just run off again. She could have told me.

The bag I'd taken from the flat was hidden under my bed, behind the box for my laptop and some old trainers that didn't fit me any more. I took it out and thought about ripping open the brown tape it was sealed with. But something stopped me, and I went back to surfing the Net. Cassie had made me promise not to open the bag and I didn't want to let her down.

But I did. I resisted for another hour and then I *had* to open the bag. The more I thought about it, the more it did my head in. In the end I gave in. The bag was wrapped up tight, so it took a while to get the tape off. I went and got some scissors to help. Inside the first bag was a second one, and inside that a third. At last the stuff inside fell out and I got confused. There was a DVD with no label on it, a pink hairbrush, a silver bracelet with two bunny charms on it, and a pair of yellow knickers. I looked at them again

and again, trying to work things out. I was stuck.
What the Hell was going on?

That night, I had the worst dream I'd ever
had. I was standing in the park, looking down
at the brook, when Cassie called out my name.
I turned but I couldn't see her. Her voice got
louder and louder, but I couldn't see where
she was. My ears started to buzz. The ground
around my feet began to cave in and soon I was
falling down into the dark. I called out, yelled
and shouted, but it was no good. I thought I was
going to die and I closed my eyes. Only I didn't
die. I opened my eyes and saw that I was in a
strange bedroom. The walls were painted soft
pink and the bed was covered in a yellow duvet
with bright pink flowers. On the ceiling someone
had painted the moon and some stars. There was
music playing, some boy band I'd never heard
before. I could smell fresh bread, like when it's
just been taken out of the oven. And then I saw
Cassie.

She was standing in front of a mirror, and
I called out to her. When she didn't reply, I got
off the bed and stood behind her. Her reflection
smiled back at me. But she looked sick. Her
hair was limp and greasy and her cheeks were

hollow. Streaks of grey dirt covered her forehead and neck. A fly crawled past her right ear and into her hair. I tried to brush the fly away but I missed. Cassie began to giggle and asked if I wanted a kiss. I heard myself say yes.

And then I watched her turn towards me ...

Her eyes were just black holes. Thousands of tiny worms crawled out of her mouth, nose and ears. She began to pull her hair out in huge clumps. She opened her mouth, spat out more worms ...

And then she howled at me ...

I woke up screaming and covered in sweat. My mum ran into the room and grabbed hold of my shoulders.

"Sam! Sam!" she shouted. "What's the matter – are you sick?"

I heard myself mumble but didn't understand the words I was using. My mum began to shake me.

"Sam!" she screamed.

The words began to make sense. I was repeating what Cassie had said to me about the contents of the bag.

"*Don't watch it! Don't watch it!*"

My mum hugged me and told me I was OK.

"It's just a nightmare," she said. "Just a bad dream. You're safe now, Sam."

At last I realised what was going on and pulled myself free.

"I'm fine," I said. "Honest, Mum."

My mum looked at me in concern.

"What happened?" she asked. "You haven't had a dream like that since ..."

And then it hit me – a wave of sickness that nearly turned my stomach inside out. I looked at my mum and started to cry.

"Sam?" she asked. "What's the matter?"

"I'm so stupid!" I shouted back. "*STUPID, STUPID, STUPID!*"

"You're scaring me," my mum sobbed. "Stop, Sam!"

I didn't listen to her. I kept on shouting at myself. My mum tried to cover my mouth with her hand. Tears were streaming down her face.

"SAM!!!"

I stopped suddenly and sat back in my bed.

"I'm sorry," I told her. "It was just a dream."

"But you called yourself stupid. Why did you do that?" she asked.

"I *am* stupid," I said, trying to think of a lie. "I mean, I was crying like some baby. I'm fifteen."

My mum stroked my face with her hand. She looked relieved.

"You're not stupid," she told me. "People have bad dreams all the time. And there's nothing wrong with crying."

"Doesn't matter," I said. "I'm OK now."

My mum gave me a funny look as she wiped away my tears.

"Are you sure?" she asked, looking at the clock by my bed. "Do you want me to call the doctor or anything? You scared me."

"I'm sorry, Mum," I said. "It was just a really, really bad dream. I'm fine now. Promise."

"You're sure?"

"Yeah. You need to get to work."

Mum fussed over me some more before she left. As soon as the door slammed shut, I sprang out of bed and pulled out the bag. I emptied the stuff onto my bed and picked up the DVD. My nightmare had been telling me something – something I already knew. I just hadn't seen it, that's all. It was hidden away in the back of my mind.

I took the DVD into the living room and put it into the cheap player my uncle had bought for us. The disc took a while to load but when it did, it played automatically. What it showed me made my blood freeze ...

Chapter 10
Screams

The DVD showed a dark room that I didn't recognise. Someone was behind the camera, out of shot. They were adjusting the lens, zooming in and out on a bed. Then the screen went black for a minute. When the video started again, I saw a pair of bare legs kicking on the bed. I couldn't see anything else of the person they belonged to except for a pair of yellow knickers. It was a girl.

A man's voice spoke on the video.

"There, there," it said. "No need to cry ... Ssh!"

I heard the girl whimper and cry.

"Be a good girl and I'll make sure you enjoy yourself," the man said.

I started to feel sick. I paused the disc and ran into my bedroom to grab my laptop. I brought it back to the living room and booted it up. It took ages to get going and I felt like I was going out of my mind. How could I have been so stupid?

When the laptop was ready, I went straight to Google. The search was almost instant. I read down the results until I saw what I wanted. I clicked on the link and the local BBC news page opened up. The photo it showed made my hands start to shake ...

I turned back to the DVD and pressed play on the remote. The man in the video carried on speaking to the girl. Then I saw him enter the frame. He was naked and flabby around the middle. I hit fast-forward, and looked away. I knew what he was about to do. The video whizzed past each frame, so fast that I couldn't see what was happening. And I didn't want to see. I wanted to run and hide. My mouth went so dry that I thought I was going to puke. I looked down at my shaky hands and shook my head. Was I completely stupid?

I pressed play and watched the man cover the girl with a dirty blanket. Then he turned to the camera and grinned. I knew then why Cassie hadn't come back. She wasn't *ever* going to come back ...

See, the girl on the video was dead. She was the same girl whose face stared back at me from my laptop. A beautiful, pale-skinned teenager, with bright red hair and sparkling emerald eyes. The girl staring back at me was ... Cassie.

But if you think that was the worst thing, you'd be wrong. The worst thing – the thing that made me scream?

The man in the video ...

... was my dad.

Our books are tested
for children and young people by
children and young people.

Thanks to everyone who consulted on
a manuscript for their time and effort in
helping us to make our books better
for our readers.